T0199057

Traveling
Through the Woods

LaShonda Epps

Illustrations by Antoine Epps

Print information available on the last page

Rev. date: 04/21/2017

To order additional copies of this book, contact:
Xlibris
1-888-795-4274
www.Xlibris.com
Orders@Xlibris.com

Traveling Through the Woods

There once were eight little animals traveling through the woods on their own.They all entered the woods at different times, so they were unaware of each other. The name of the woods was Sweet Freedom Village. While they walked through, they all found comfy little habitats that they could make their own. So they made their homes right there, in the middle of the woods. It was quiet, and seemed like no other animals lived close by. Little did they know that other animals were thinking the same exact thing, moving in on that very same day.

The animals that found their new homes in the woods that day were Keela the bird, Sugar Bear the big bear, Honey Bear the medium bear, Teddy the little bear, Puffy the squirrel, Reacko the raccoon, Squeaky the mouse, and Pecko the possum.

Each morning the animals woke up to the beautiful sunshine. They took baths and ventured off to find food. They all visited the same wateringhole every day, but never ran into each other. Eventually, all the eight animals happened to meet at the waterhole, one hot summer afternoon. They all got along just fine, and became the best of friends.

They all agreed to meet at the waterhole the same time each day, so they could get to know each other better. They started having sleepovers, eating together and play dates. They soon found that the longer they stayed at the waterhole, the more other animals they met, coming in and out of Sweet Freedom Village. They also found that there were many other animals living in the same woods that they were living in.

Those eight animals got to know just about everything about each other. They learned each other's names, birthdays, where they came from, and what their favorite foods were. Each of the friends was everyone's favorite. No one was less liked than the other. They loved being around each other so much that they came up with a cool name for their group. They called themselves the SVP (Sweet Village Pak), after the name of the woods they all stayed in.

The SVP decided to throw a party for all the animals that lived in the village, including all the ones that just visited the woods every day. The SVP wanted to get to know every animal that came through the woods. They threw the biggest party Sweet Freedom Village had ever seen. That was the longest night they had ever had. They had so much fun and met so many new animals; they enjoyed everything so much that come morning of the next day all of them forgot their best friend's birthday.

It was Sugar Bear's birthday but nobody remembered. The big party from the night before had everyone tired and thinking about everything else besides the next celebration. Sugar Bear was the only one thinking of his birthday, all day and what to do next. He didn't want to tell any of his friends because he wanted it to be special. He wanted his friends to remember his birthday on their own. He was sad, but went on with his day walking around searching for honey and picking berries. As Sugar Bear walked through the woods he bumped into some of his friends. He asked them, "Is today a special day?" Everyone said, "No, why do you ask?" Sugar Bear didn't tell them why he had asked or even that it was his birthday. He was just hoping that they would figure it out on their own or had something planned for him already.

Later that day Sugar was still walking around Sweet Freedom Village thinking to himself; just because we had that big bash yesterday don't mean that they should forget my birthday for today! Sugar Bear thought and walked so much that he missed their daily meeting at the wateringhole; all the other members of the SVP were there, and wondering why Sugar didn't show up. They stayed there and waited and talked, and then they finally figured out that it was Sugar's birthday. They were all shocked, "How could we all forget it was Sugar Bear's birthday!?" "Sugar must be upset and disappointed!" Keela said. So the SVP got the whole village together to throw a big birthday party for Sugar.

They had fun getting the secret party together for Sugar. They all brought presents, prizes, and food. Keela brought the tasty salty seeds. Reacko brought the sandwiches. Honey Bear was happy to bring the honey since that was his favorite dish. He had enough to share with the whole village. Teddy brought the berries and a big bowl of sugar to go with it, since he knew that's what Sugar Bear loved the most. Puffy brought his favorite kind of nuts to share. Squeaky brought all the cheese and jam anyone could want. While Peacko ran home and made a tall cake with all kinds of fruits and filling.

They were all running back and forth from the waterhole getting everything set up. "But there's another side to this party", Teddy said. They all asked "And what's that!" "We have to get Sugar Bear here!" "Oh yeah!!" They all replied. They needed someone to go and get him, someone who was fast and would be able to spot him walking around through the trees. Keela said, "I'll go, I can fly quickly then get him to come to the wateringhole". "We will be here setting up the party while waiting", Honey Bear said happily. Reacko shouted, "Let's hurry up before they come back"!

Soon enough they got done setting up the surprise. They even had time to run and hide. Meanwhile Keela found Sugar, still walking through the woods. Keela said "Sugar, Sugar Bear!! Come quick, I have something I have to show you now"!! "What is it", he responded nervously and excitedly because he didn't know what was going on. Keela just started flying fast, dodging in and out of the tree branches. So Sugar ran quickly right behind her, to follow where she was flying to.

They made it to the party just in time.

"Here you are" Keela announced.

HAPPY BIRTHDAY SUGAR BEAR!!!!!

"So you all didn't forget my, my birthday after all didn't you"!? "Oh I'm so happy", Sugar Bear said, he was so surprised; he really thought all of his friends forgot all about his special day. They partied with music, food, games, and delicious cake all night long. Everyone helped clean up and didn't go home until after midnight. The entire SVP and the rest of the village lived happily ever after. They continued to throw big bashes all the time. They all stayed the best of friends in the quiet little woods of Sweet Freedom Village.

Printed in the United States
By Bookmasters